ALSO BY TEVIN HANSEN

Junkyard Adventures

Word Dragon

Sea Serpent of Science

Giant of Geography

Alien of Astronomy

Mermaid of Music

Art Monster

Gargoyle of Geometry

Weather Witch

Mummy of Medicine

Math Dragon

Hairytale Adventures

The Birthday Bear

The Museum Guide

The Zookeeper

Halloween Adventures

The Halloween Grump

The Haunted Hospital

The Halloween Space Adventure

MatH Dragon

Handersen Publishing, LLC
Lincoln, Nebraska

Junkyard Adventure #10
Math Dragon

Library of Congress Cataloging-in-Publication Data

Names: Hansen, Tevin, author.
Title: Math dragon / Tevin Hansen.
Description: Lincoln, Nebraska : Handersen Publishing, LLC, [2022] |
   Series: Junkyard adventures ; #10 | Audience: Ages 6-9. |
   Audience: Grades 2-3. | Summary: Siblings Eli and Grace travel
   to a dragon's home and go deep inside a mountain, where they
   search for treasure and solve a series of math riddles.
Identifiers: LCCN 2022021042 (print) | LCCN 2022021043 (ebook)
   | ISBN 9781647030698 (paperback) | ISBN 9781647030704
   (hardback) | ISBN 9781647030711 (epub)
Subjects: CYAC: Dragons--Fiction. | Riddles--Fiction. | Mathematics--
   Fiction. | Brothers and sisters--Fiction. | Adventure and
   adventurers--Fiction. | LCGFT: Action and adventure fiction. |
   Novels.
Classification: LCC PZ7.1.H36433 Mat 2022 (print) | LCC
   PZ7.1.H36433 (ebook) | DDC [Fic]--dc23
LC record available at https://lccn.loc.gov/2022021042
LC ebook record available at https://lccn.loc.gov/2022021043

Publisher Website: www.HandersenPublishing.com
Publisher Email: editors@HandersenPublishing.com
Author Website: www.TevinHansen.com
Artist Website: loweart.portfoliobox.net

A JUNKYARD ADVENTURE

Ma+H Dragon

Tevin Hansen

Handersen Publishing, LLC
Lincoln, Nebraska

Meet Uncle Larry

The junk store on Broadway Street had a million things for sale. And the man who owned the shop had a million stories to tell.

His name was Uncle Larry.

The sign out front…

Uncle Larry's Antique Shop

…wasn't a complete lie.

There really were antiques inside his store. There were old lamps, paintings with fancy wood frames, art sculptures, baseball and hockey cards, jewelry and furniture, old collectible toys, and lots of other things.

The junkyard was out back.

Uncle Larry had a bunch of junky old cars and trucks that would cost so much to fix that it was cheaper to buy a new one.

Uncle Larry's store also had some of the coolest stuff on the planet. Decades worth of junk and antiques were packed, racked, and stacked into his crowded old shop on Broadway. His apartment was just above the store.

Uncle Larry was a friendly old man who loved to sell things and talk to people. He never married, and never had any children, but he loved to tell stories to kids while their parents shopped in his store.

If it was okay with their moms or dads, or whoever the kids were out shopping with, Uncle Larry would grab his old brown leather stool, plunk right down in the middle of the store, and tell a story.

Uncle Larry had a million stories to tell.

And they always came true.

1

Eli's Gift

Beep! Beep! Beep!

Eli's alarm had been going off for several minutes before he rolled over to turn it off. Then he lay back down on his pillow.

A voice said, "Told you not to stay up so late."

"AHH!" Eli sat up quickly when he found his sister sitting at the edge of his bed. She was waiting for him to get up.

"Can you please knock?" said Eli, his heart still racing. "You scared me."

Grace folded her arms. "I did knock," she told him. "Three times. But you still didn't wake up. You shouldn't have stayed up so late playing video games last night."

Eli yawned. "Hey, I also read my new book for almost an hour," he said, defending himself. "Dad told me I could stay up a little later because it's my birthday. But you're right—" He yawned again. "That was way too late."

Grace told him she'd been up for over an hour, eating breakfast, drawing, and helping their dad get things ready for the party.

Eli kicked off the blankets. There was no way he could go back to sleep now. Especially when this was such a special occasion. Today was his 10th birthday!

"So?" said Grace.

"So what?" said Eli sleepily. His hair was sticking up at funny angles, and his head was still full of images from his strange dream—a dragon dream. Two huge dragons were playing a strange game of baseball. They smashed giant rocks and used their powerful tails like a bat.

Grace sighed. "Are you going to open it? Go on, let's see what it is!" She pointed to the small package on his bedside table, where it had been sitting for weeks. They were both excited to see what it was. Especially since it had come from Uncle Larry's store.

"Okay, okay..." Eli grabbed the package off the messy bedside table, full of books and piles of junk. He was also curious about the present wrapped in plain white paper.

"I'll bet it's something really good," said Grace as she watched him tear off the wrapping paper.

And it *was* something really good. Just not what either of them expected.

"The astrolabe?" said Grace, surprised.

The gift Eli held in his hand wasn't much bigger than a compass or an antique pocket watch. The brass metal needed a good polish, but the letters, numbers, and symbols were clearly visible.

"Cool," said Eli. "My very own astrolabe. I just wish I knew how to use it."

Grace shrugged. "I wonder why Uncle Larry

gave it to you?" she said. "Maybe he wants you to learn about stars and the solar system instead of staying up late and playing video games."

Eli glared at her. "Ha-ha, very funny." But he was curious too. Why would he need an old instrument that could be used like a sundial, figure out what time the moon will rise, or could help map out the stars?

There was no time to figure it out because their dad was calling to them from downstairs.

"I could use some help down here!" hollered Dad. "Today is somebody's birthday—that is, if he ever gets up."

"Coming, Dad!" said Eli, then he and his sister raced downstairs to help out.

"There's the birthday boy!" Dad gave Eli a bone-squishing hug. "The big one-oh."

Dad handed him a balloon. "I hope your lungs are ready to blow up all these balloons."

Eli asked, "Can I have breakfast first?"

Dad laughed. "Yes, go ahead. But then we've got some work to do. The party starts at two o'clock. We still need to decorate the backyard, clean up the house a little bit, and pick the cake up from the store."

A few minutes later, with his stomach full of cereal, Eli was helping blow up balloons with everyone else. They hadn't gotten very far when their dad's phone rang. Eli and Grace listened from the living room.

"Oh, hi..."

"Yes, they're both here..."

"Today? Well, I suppose..."

"Okay, bye."

Dad came back into the living room with a cup of coffee in one hand, and a half filled balloon in the other. He set down his cup and finished blowing up the balloon, but the effort looked like it was giving him a headache.

"Who was that on the phone, Dad?" asked Eli, even though he had a pretty good idea.

"Hm? Oh, that was Professor Harvard," said Dad. "He called to see if we could swing by the store today." He grabbed another balloon, but had to take a break after just a few breaths.

Eli and Grace stared at him, waiting.

"I told him today might be difficult because it's your birthday," Dad went on. "But maybe…"

"What, Dad?" asked Grace.

"Well, let's see—" Dad checked his watch before answering. "He told me it wouldn't take too long, and that it would really help him out."

Eli and Grace stood up, ready to go.

Dad let the air deflate from his balloon. "Maybe we can buy some kind of hand pump to use on all these balloons." He looked at his two kids, who weren't properly dressed for an outing. "And you two can't go out still dressed in your PJs."

Thump-thump-thump-thump-thump.

Eli and Grace raced upstairs to their bedrooms. They got dressed, brushed their teeth, and were back downstairs in less than five minutes.

Dad jiggled the car keys. "Ready?"

"Ready!" they both said.

Going to Uncle Larry's store on his birthday made it seem extra special. The only strange part was that the keys to the store were hanging on the hook next to the garage door.

Eli picked up the red shoelace with the keys to Uncle Larry's store and handed them to Grace.

"Here, sis," said Eli. "You carry them this time. The note Harvard left us said these keys were for both of us."

Grace smiled as she placed the lanyard full of keys around her neck. But there was a sad look behind her eyes. During their last junkyard adventure, Uncle Larry had disappeared in a flash of bright light while trying to help them.

This time, they hoped Uncle Larry was back.

2
Battle Horn

When the family SUV pulled into the parking lot about twenty minutes later, another car was just leaving. It was already past 10 o'clock in the morning, so the store should've been open. But the **OPEN** sign hadn't been turned around, so the store looked like it was still **CLOSED**.

"Remember, we can't stay long," said Dad, shutting off the engine. "Just a quick visit to see what Professor Harvard wants. Then we have some birthday errands to run, okay?"

"Okay, Dad."

Everyone piled out of the car and walked up

to the front door. While their dad knocked for someone to let them in, Eli and Grace peeked through the dirty window. The glass hadn't been cleaned in years, so it was hard to see inside.

Everything appeared normal. Shelves, tables, and every bit of space was filled with antiques and junk—the same as it always was. But nobody was there to let them inside.

Dad checked his watch. "That's strange," he said. "It's almost ten-thirty, but the store is still closed."

Grace rattled the keys that hung around her neck. "But we can still get in, right?"

Dad let out a heavy sigh. "Technically, yes, but I'm not sure that's a good idea," he said. "Where's Professor Harvard? He told us to stop by the store, but he's not even in there."

Grace remembered which key to use from the last time, so she had the front door open in a matter of seconds.

Da-ding! Da-ding!

The familiar sound of the doorbell rang out,

but quickly fizzled out with a dull *zuzz-zuzz-zuzz* sound.

Clunk.

The door buzzer fell off the door. It crashed to the floor, broke into several pieces, then lay silent.

"Uh-oh," said Dad, picking it up. "We'll have to tell Larry about this. I hope we don't get charged for it. This old doorbell looks like an antique."

The store was unusually quiet today. No customers, no soft music playing on the antique record player, and no sounds of Uncle Larry tripping over his own feet and accidentally breaking something valuable.

Dad hollered, "Uncle Larry? Professor Harvard?" He paused. "Is anyone here?"

All three of them walked up to the main counter. They expected to see the store owner sitting on his favorite leather stool, reading a newspaper, or digging through the piles of junk to find something he'd lost.

Nobody was behind the counter—or anywhere else. It was just the three of them in the store.

"There's a note," said Eli, pointing to the funny looking horn with a yellow sticky note attached to it: Ring for service!

The horn was encrusted with jewels, fancy designs, and an orange price tag.

Battle Horn 17th century
Estimated value:
$22,500

Dad carefully picked up the horn and gave it a try. He didn't do so well at getting it to make the proper sound, so he handed it over to Eli.

Eli took a deep breath, then blew the battle horn as loud as he could.

Da-Da-DAAAAAH!

The horn bellowed a deep, long note that rang throughout the entire store. It was so loud that Grace had to cover her ears.

"Nice job, Eli!" Dad gave his son a pat on the shoulder. "You did much better than me."

Shortly after the battle cry from the centuries-old horn bellowed through the aisles, a different kind of sound came from the back of the store.

Footsteps.

But not *human* footsteps.

3
Party Supplies

What sounded like the paws of a large dog were coming down one of the aisles. Those padded footsteps quickly changed to the sound of a person walking toward them.

"Eli and Grace!" said a familiar voice. "I'm so glad you could make it."

It was Professor Harvard. He'd changed from a playful Golden Retriever into his regular human form. He wore the same old gray sweater, with his long hair and scruffy beard full of dust, sand, and what looked like bits of rock.

"Hi, Harvard!" said Eli.

"You're back!" said Grace.

Harvard greeted the kids excitedly, then shook hands with their dad. He'd been away on junkyard business for a while, so nobody had seen him in weeks.

"Good to see you again, Professor," said Dad. "We tried knocking on the door, but nobody answered. I hope it's okay if we, um…sort of let ourselves in."

Grace held up the keys. "Here you go!"

"That's perfectly fine," said Harvard, though he didn't bother to take the keys. "Why don't you hang on to those, Grace. I'm not sure that our dear Uncle Larry will need them back."

The store grew quiet for a moment.

"Oh, I see. Is Larry retiring?" asked Dad.

Harvard took a long time to answer. "I'm not sure what Larry has planned," he admitted. "All I know is that he's having a wonderful time, off enjoying the sights. Larry's been running this store for a long, long time, so I think he's earned some time off."

"Well, good for him," said Dad, nodding his approval. He was the only one who looked happy.

Eli and Grace were glad to hear that Uncle Larry was safe—wherever he was. They just hoped their days of junkyard adventures weren't over.

Harvard noticed their sad faces. "No, no, no," he said kindly. "This is not a day to be sad. This is a day to celebrate! Have you got everything you need for the party?"

Dad shook his head. "Not exactly," he admitted. "We could probably use some more paper plates, plastic utensils, and we still need to find a party supply store because we forgot to buy gift bags for the guests."

Eli gave a little cough. "We?"

"Dad, it was on our list," said Grace, giving her dad a stern look. "Eli and I didn't forget. *You* did."

Dad laughed. "Okay, okay," he said with his hands in the air. "I forgot the gift bags. You two did put it on the list. I just forgot to bring the list with me."

Harvard raised his eyebrows. "Gift bags?" He opened his arms wide. "Then you came to the right place! You might want to take a quick look down aisle twenty-five, where we have a nice selection of slightly used and discount party supplies. Just arrived this morning!" He winked at Eli and Grace, who recognized the sparkle behind his dark brown eyes.

Eli turned to his dad. "Do we have time to go on a quick junkyard ad—" He stopped before saying *junkyard adventure*. "I mean, listen to a quick story?"

Grace squeezed her hands together. "*Pleeease*, Dad? Just one really fast story for Eli's birthday. Please, please, please?"

Neither of them let up. They ganged up on their dad until he finally agreed to let them stay.

"Okay, but make it quick," warned Dad. "We have a lot to do before the guests start arriving at two o'clock. We have to set up the games, get the picnic table ready, and we still have a ton of balloons to blow up."

Harvard was impressed. "Sounds like it's going to be a wonderful birthday party," he said. "We have some used outdoor games the kids might enjoy. And I believe we have a few gently used plastic table cloths."

Dad was already heading toward the party supply aisle, hoping to get a few things knocked off their list. "I shouldn't be more than a few minutes!" he hollered over his shoulder. "Meet back at the checkout in ten minutes, okay?"

Eli and Grace shouted, "Okay, Dad!"

Harvard leaned down to whisper, "And that should be all the time we need..." He spun on his heels and headed for the back of the store, where a sign was hanging above an old wooden door.

Junkyard Adventures

4
Magic in a Cup

When they were just about to round the corner leading to the junkyard door, Harvard stopped. He put a hand to his ear, listening carefully. Eli and Grace stood there quietly and listened too. All they could hear was their dad, whistling while he looked at the party supplies on the other side of the store.

Tink.

A small noise came from nearby. It sounded like something hitting the tile floor.

"Ah—so close." Harvard snapped his finger as if he'd guessed wrong. "Must be the next aisle over."

As soon as they peeked around the corner of the next aisle…

"That must be your first magic item," said Harvard, pointing at the floor. "An interesting one, since it could change into something else—or remain the same."

On the floor was a triple-A battery.

Eli kneeled down to pick it up right when a second battery rolled off the shelf. This one landed on the back of his head.

Clunk.

"Ow!" cried Eli.

Grace tried not to laugh. "Are you okay?"

"Yes, I'm okay." Eli rubbed his head.

Harvard said, "I'm afraid the magic junk in this store can be a little mischievous."

When Eli pocketed the two batteries, a rattling noise made him jump. On the shelf behind them was a set of dusty old goblets with an orange price tag.

19th Century Victorian
(Sterling silver)
$1300/set of 4

Clink, clink.

Something was moving around inside one of the cups, as if it was trying to get out.

"Forget it," said Eli, stepping back. "I'm not getting hit again. Grace, you look."

Grace cautiously tipped over the silver cup that was dancing on the shelf, then peeked inside.

"It's okay, Eli," she said. "Nothing to worry about. It's just this tiny thing." She held up a small, metal bit that could fit into the end of a multi-use screwdriver.

Eli shrugged. "Sure, why not," he said. "Maybe we'll use some tools to build something on this adventure."

"We could build a dance studio!" said Grace with her eyes sparkling. "Then I can practice ballet whenever I want."

Harvard put a finger to his lips. "Keep listening," he whispered. "There could be more magic junk. Or perhaps you'll only need those few things." He tapped a finger to his forehead. "And, of course, your knowledge to get through this adventure."

Everyone listened for the sound of more magic junk rattling around on the shelves. All they heard was a voice on the other end of the store say, "Yes! Gift bags! This store really does have everything."

Harvard looked pleased. "See? I told your dad it would be a good idea to stop by today." He winked, then waved at them to follow him to the back of the store.

"Grace, come on!" said Eli. "Hurry up!"

"I'm coming!" Grace paused to scoop up the piece of string she saw laying in the center of the aisle, then hurried to catch up with her brother.

With their magic junk stuffed in their pockets, Eli and Grace stood at the open door. There was nothing outside except the same old rusty cars, trucks with no engine, stacks of used appliances, and a ton of other junk. They were ready to step through the door and begin their adventure! But there was one more surprise waiting for them at the back of the store.

Harvard was coming along too.

5
Special Gifts

"You're coming with us?" Eli moved over to make room. This was the first time that a grownup had gone with them. Uncle Larry would usually just wave goodbye, then hurry off to deal with the customers. It would be nice to have a helpful guide come along—especially Harvard, who invented the magical world of junkyard adventures.

Harvard took a deep breath. "I think you might need me on this adventure," he told them. "I may be able to provide a good distraction."

Eli and Grace were excited to go. But Harvard didn't seem too happy that he was tagging along on this adventure.

"As you know, I've been away for a while," said Harvard. "Dealing with Fireball and Lasher has proven to be a rather difficult case of sibling rivalry."

Grace's eyes grew wide. "They're brothers?"

Harvard shook his head. "Brother and sister," he explained. "Lasher, the eldest, believes that numbers are the greatest. Her younger brother, Fireball, insists that words are more important."

Grace scrunched up her eyebrows and twitched her lips side to side like she sometimes did when she was thinking really hard.

"Aren't they equal?" she said. "Words and numbers are both important, right? Neither one of them is better than the other."

Eli thought the exact same thing. "Words help us communicate," he said. "But without numbers, we couldn't count, tell the time, or use a calendar."

Grace gave a small laugh. "And nobody would know which day was their birthday," she said, then gave her brother a nudge with her elbow.

Harvard threw his hands in the air. "I agree completely," he said. "And that's what I have been telling them for years. But still, they have made it perfectly clear that they will not assist me with any more junkyard adventures until the matter is settled once and for all."

Eli and Grace weren't sure how they could help Harvard, though they definitely wanted to give it a try.

"I've called several meetings with the other teachers you've met during your adventures," Harvard went on. "That's when your names came up."

Eli and Grace listened closely, while also trying to dream up a way to finally put an end to the pointless argument of words versus numbers.

They were both stumped for ideas.

"A close friend of mine told me that you two might be able to finally put an end to their silly argument," explained Harvard.

"Us?" said Eli, confused. "I don't know how to stop two dragons from arguing."

Harvard scratched his scruffy beard. "It seems that our friend Torus believes you two have a rare, special gift," he went on. "The gargoyle of geometry is a genius when it comes to shapes, so I can only assume that it has something to do with the subject of math."

Eli shuffled his feet. "I'm okay at math," he said. "I do pretty well at school. Grace does too."

Grace nodded that it was true. "I like math."

Harvard let out a tired sigh. "Well, you're about to meet a math dragon," he said. "So maybe this 'special gift' you have will finally put an end to their silly argument."

Before they stepped through the junkyard door, a voice called across the store.

"Hey, Harvard?"

"Yes, Ben?"

"You don't happen to have a balloon pump for sale, do you?" asked their dad. "We have a few bags of balloons back at the house that need to be inflated. The first couple of balloons I blew up gave me a terrible headache."

Clunk.

A noise echoed through the store. Something had just arrived on one of the shelves.

"As a matter of fact, I believe we do," shouted Harvard. "Check near the end of the aisle. If you don't see it there, check near the front counter—underneath the mess!"

Eli and Grace giggled. The mess that Uncle Larry had up at the front counter took years to create—and held many secrets.

Harvard rubbed his hands together. "Ready?"

"Ready," said Eli and Grace.

Together, all three of them stepped through the junkyard door. There was a bright flash, like somebody pulling back the curtain of a dark room and letting in the sunshine. And then—

Whoosh!

They were gone.

6
Desert Mountains

After their eyes adjusted to the bright light, Eli and Grace took in the amazing scenery. A wide open area spread out for miles. There were plenty of boulders, funny shaped trees, and lots of strange cactus plants with bright flowers growing out of them.

"This place is cool," said Eli, spinning around in a circle. "Mountains and desert. You could ride a dune buggy in those sand dunes over there, then go mountain climbing in the same day."

"In the same hour," said Grace. "I'll bet we could walk to either one in just a few minutes."

Rugged mountains were on the left, stretching way up into the blue sky. To the right side were great hills of smooth sand that rose hundreds of feet in the air.

"Welcome to the Desert Mountains," said Harvard. "Where dragons live—and play."

Ka-BOOM.

The ground shook.

"Um, what was that?" asked Grace, worried. "Was that an earthquake?"

Eli was wondering the same thing. "Sounded more like an explosion."

Harvard held up one hand to shield his eyes from the bright sun. "Oh, nothing to worry about," he said calmly. "Just a friendly game of dragonball."

"*Ack!*" Eli accidentally swallowed his gum when he heard this news. "Professor Harvard, did you just say…*dragonball*?" It sounded very similar to the strange dream he'd had last night.

Harvard nodded like it was no big deal. "The game is similar to baseball," he explained.

"Except dragonball uses a much bigger ball, and a tail instead of a bat. Dragonball is also much more dangerous than regular baseball."

Eli couldn't tell who looked more worried—his sister, or *him*. The explosions were as loud as the biggest fireworks set off on July 4th.

BOOM.

"Looks like Fireball and Lasher have stopped arguing long enough to play a few rounds of dragonball," said Harvard, pointing off in the distance. "Look over there, in between those two cliffs."

Shielding their eyes from the sun, Eli and Grace could make out where the sloping mountains changed into steep cliffs. Two walls of rock that were big enough to hide whatever was causing the explosions.

BOOM.

With a gleam in his eye, Harvard said, "Race you there!" He changed into his other form—a Golden Retriever with shaggy blonde hair, wagging tongue, and bluish-brown eyes. The friendly dog gave one happy bark, then took off running toward the sound of the explosions.

"Harvard, wait!" Eli chased after the dog, but quickly gave up because he was nowhere near as fast as a speedy canine.

"It's okay, Eli," said Grace. "We can walk over there. It doesn't look too far."

Together, they followed after the dog. They had to be careful on the tricky terrain. With so many holes to make them stumble, and a ton of rocks to slip on, somebody could get hurt. There were lots of hiding spots for all sorts of desert creatures.

"I hope there aren't any rattlesnakes," said Eli, stepping carefully over a small hole.

Grace gasped. "Why did you have to say that?"

"Sorry," said Eli, feeling bad for even bringing up the subject of *snakes*. They walked in silence for a while, helping each other along the way.

Less than ten minutes later, they made it to the cliffs. It wasn't until they got much closer that the explosions started back up again.

BOOM!

As soon as they rounded the corner, Eli and Grace suddenly stopped. Neither of them could believe what they saw standing there.

Two dragons.

The green dragon was standing behind a wooden catapult that was bigger than *he* was. And this was no small dragon!

The purple dragon, quite a bit larger than the first, was up to bat. But the second dragon wasn't holding a bat like players do in a proper baseball game. The dragon was using its powerful tail to smash the boulders that went sailing through the air at least a hundred feet high, then came down near home base.

Ka-BOOM!

7
Dragonball

Professor Harvard stood safely behind the wooden catapult. As soon as he saw Eli and Grace walk around the corner of the steep cliff, he waved at them to come over.

Fireball's purple and gold eyes lit up when he saw who came running toward them.

"Eli and Grace!" said Fireball in his deep voice. "How are you? It's been far too long since I've seen you both."

"Hi, Fireball!" Grace ran up and wrapped her small arms around the dragon's massive leg. She did the best she could, but trying to hug a dragon wasn't an easy thing to do.

Eli waved to his old friend with scaly green skin and huge purple wings. "Today's my birthday," he told the dragon. "The big one-oh. Double digits!"

"So I hear," said Fireball excitedly. His eyes gleamed in the sun. "Ten years old! How wonderful. I remember when I turned ten, such a long, long time ago."

Another deep voice said, "I'm *waaaaiting*!"

The dragon who'd been using its strong tail like a baseball bat was now stomping its large foot on the ground, awaiting another boulder.

Fireball let out such a heavy sigh that smoke wafted out from the corners of his mouth. "You'll have to excuse my sister," he said apologetically. "She's in a bad M-O-O-D. We've been having a bit of an argument lately."

Thump, thump, thump.

"Hurry up! Toss a boulder, will you?" said the dragon with scaly purple skin and green wings. She was ready for the next pitch.

"Okay, my dear sister," said Fireball calmly. "I'm loading the next rock now. See?"

With his strong, scaly arms, Fireball selected a rock the size of a small car. The boulder must have weighed several thousand pounds! But Fireball picked it up like it was a normal sized baseball. Then he carefully placed it inside the huge pouch, attached by thick ropes.

"This is called a *trebuchet*," explained Fireball.

"A *treb-you-chet*?" repeated Grace. "It looks like a really big catapult."

The pouch was attached to a long sling that launched the giant boulders.

"Everyone stay behind me, please," warned Fireball. "I don't want anyone getting hurt during this silly game that my sister likes so much. Me?" He winked, then whispered, "I'd much rather play a civilized game of Scrabble."

They watched as the mighty dragon pulled down the *counterweight*, a huge wooden box filled with sand. When everything was locked in place, it was time to launch the boulder.

Wham! Wham!

Lasher smacked her tail on the ground,

then she got into position the same way the professional baseball players do.

"Eli?"

"Yes, Fireball?"

"Since today is your birthday," said the dragon, "would you like to do the honors?"

Eli happily agreed. "Just pull the rope?"

Fireball nodded. "First, you shout...*loose*," he explained. "Then you simply pull that rope to launch the boulder. Give the rope a good, hard tug. Got it?"

Eli was nervous, but nodded. "Okay, got it."

Standing up tall, Fireball put one clawed hand to his mouth and shouted to his sister. "Lasher! Are you ready over there?"

"Yes, I'm ready!" came the quick reply from Lasher. "I've been ready for the last ten minutes and fourteen seconds!"

Grace and Harvard stood back to give Eli some room. The rope used to release the heavy boulder was close to twenty feet long.

"Loose!" shouted Eli, then pulled the rope.

Swoosh!

The trebuchet swung around, and the boulder went sailing through the air. As the huge rock went hurtling toward the dragon standing a hundred yards away, the creature's powerful tail came whipping around.

Crash!

The boulder was smashed to bits.

"Again!" shouted Lasher, ready for another one. "By my count, that's only nine hundred and ninety-nine! Let's make it an even thousand, then we'll take a short break and do some Sudoku."

Fireball waved his arms. "That was the last one!" he called to his sister. "I'll have to go collect some more rocks. But first, why don't you come over here and meet a couple of old friends!"

Lasher huffed. "Oh, fine," she grumbled. "I could use a break anyway." She was surprisingly quick on her feet for such a heavy dragon.

THUMP. THUMP. **THUMP.**

8
Ancient Argument

Despite appearing a little gruff, the math dragon was an excellent host. From a drawer built into the side of the trebuchet, she pulled out a small wooden table, three folding chairs, and a set of golden goblets that looked really valuable.

"Please, everyone sit," said Lasher, then brought out a used camping cooler with an orange price tag sticker from Uncle Larry's store—$5.00, marked down from $10.00.

"Refreshments?" Lasher offered everyone a drink from a pitcher of fresh iced tea. Then she handed out cookies for all the guests.

Eli, Grace, and Harvard all held up their glasses while Lasher carefully filled them up, not spilling a single drop.

"None for me, thanks," said Fireball, patting his large stomach. "I've got these delicious beauties!"

Crunch.

Fireball was a fire-breathing dragon, so he didn't need to drink water—or iced tea. Instead, he scooped up a handful of small rocks from the ground and happily munched away.

Eli laughed.

"What's so funny?" asked Grace.

"Oh, nothing," said Eli. "Just the fact that we're sitting in the shade, drinking iced tea and eating cookies with a couple of dragons."

Grace gestured toward their other friend who was sitting there alongside them. "And Professor Harvard," she said, "who can turn himself into a friendly dog."

Harvard was smiling underneath his shaggy beard. "Just another typical day inside a junkyard adventure," he commented, then raised his glass of iced tea.

Clink.

Everyone touched their glasses together, enjoying their morning snack.

Fireball raised one clawed hand like he'd just come up with the best idea ever.

"Does anyone want to play a game?" asked the word-loving dragon. From another hidden compartment inside the trebuchet, he produced a familiar board game. He rattled the box. "Scrabble, anyone?"

Lasher rolled her brilliant green eyes. "Instead of that word game you love so much," she said, "why don't we all work on some math equations. Long division? Algebra?"

Harvard's shoulders slumped. It wasn't hard to tell that he was upset because he was going to have to listen to the dragons' ancient argument about words versus numbers—*again.*

"I have another idea," suggested Harvard as he opened up the board game. "How about Fireball and I stay here and play a few rounds of Scrabble, while Lasher takes our guests to visit her beautiful mountain home."

Lasher waved off the idea. "They'd be bored senseless," she said. "There are only two things inside that mountain of ours."

"What are they?" asked Grace, curiously.

"Untold riches," said Lasher. "And wealth beyond measure. Rooms full of gold, endless silver treasures, and giant hills of precious gems."

Eli nearly choked on his cookie. Untold riches? Gold? Precious gems?

"I'd like to see your home," said Grace as she reached for another cookie. "That sounds fun."

Harvard approved. "And you never know..." He paused to take a sip of his drink. "These two young junkyard adventurers could find the mystery location of the smigitu."

Everything went quiet.

"Smigitu?" Fireball tapped one claw on his scaly chin, thinking very hard. "I know every word that's ever been created—even the trickiest

Scrabble words. And yet, I don't believe I've ever heard of something called a smigitu."

Harvard set down his glass so he could tell the story of this famous creation—the smigitu. An object so incredible...so amazing...that it could even capture the imagination of a dragon.

9
Magic String

"A smigitu is extremely rare," explained Professor Harvard, making sure he had the attention of the two dragons before going on. "That's because the smigitu happens to be the single most incredible gizmo in the universe."

The dragons listened carefully. One set of green eyes, the other purple, were locked on Professor Harvard as he explained more about this legendary object.

"Many astronomers have devoted their entire life to understanding the mysteries of the smigitu," Professor Harvard went on. "After all, there is no better tool to study the stars."

"Ooh, lovely!" said Fireball.

"Yes, this does sound interesting," said Lasher, who seemed very curious. "As you know, we dragons love watching the stars."

Harvard looked very pleased.

Eli and Grace had the feeling that there really was no object called a *smigitu*, and that Harvard was simply making up a story. But the two dragons were excited by the very idea of it.

"I recently heard a rumor that this precious item may actually be located inside your mountain home," said Harvard, casually sipping his iced tea. "Somewhere among all the gold, silver, and jewels."

Fireball and Lasher spoke to each other in an ancient language that only the two of them could understand. They both sounded very excited as they spoke, even though nobody at the table knew what they were saying.

"Lasher and I have agreed to look into this smigitu legend a bit further," said Fireball. "But only if Eli and Grace are up to the challenge."

Harvard rubbed his hands together. With a sparkle in his eyes, he leaned forward and asked the two young guests if they would enjoy some sightseeing.

"Perhaps a tour of the mountain," suggested Harvard. "Then a quest to find the smigitu." He winked so that only Eli and Grace saw him do it, keeping it a secret from the dragons.

"Sure," said Eli. "How?"

Lasher stood up from the table. "I believe the answer to that question is located in Grace's front pocket."

"Um, it is?" Grace searched her pockets. All she had was the tiny screwdriver bit from the dancing silver cup, along with the short piece of string she'd picked up. She wasn't even sure if the string was part of the magic junk they needed for their adventure.

"Dragons do not like to wear a harness," said Lasher. "But for safety reasons, I think it's best when flying."

Eli dribbled iced tea down his chin. "Fly?"

"Of course!" said Lasher. "It would take far too long to walk there. I can fly you both to the mountain entrance in less than two minutes. Approximately ninety seconds. Or two-point-five percent of an hour."

Eli and Grace were definitely up for a quest, even if flying on a dragon sounded a bit scary.

Lasher smiled. "Ah, the measurement of time," she said wistfully. "Without numbers, we wouldn't be able to tell the time at all!"

Fireball groaned. "Oh, please don't start that same old argument again." He was already setting up the Scrabble board, ready to play a game with Harvard.

Grace held up the string. "Here it is," she said. "But how is this going to help us?"

Zing!

Eli ducked his head as the string shot out of his sister's hand. The small piece of string doubled... tripled...and quadrupled in thickness and length. And it kept growing! The string grew into a strong rope that wrapped and coiled itself around the body of the dragon.

Fff-whap!

Like the sound of a whip, the string had magically turned into a riding harness, made of rope and leather. It looked similar to the saddle of a horse—except much bigger.

Lasher knelt down and allowed the two kids to climb onto her back. Eli helped his sister get into the back saddle, then he climbed up front. There were no seatbelts, only a leather rein.

"Ready to fly?" asked Lasher.

Eli was too stunned to speak, so Grace had to give him a little push to snap him out of it.

"Yeah. Um. Sorry," said Eli, shaking his head. "We're ready. I think—?" He wondered if anyone could tell how nervous he was. Or how fast his heart was racing. Or how heavy he was breathing. His sweaty hands picked up the reins, then Lasher flapped her great wings.

Whump-whump.

It was time to ride a dragon.

10
Grand Entrance

Lasher flapped her powerful wings a few more times, then her clawed feet left the ground.

"Whoa!" cried Eli, trying to keep his balance. As soon as they took to the air, it wasn't hard to tell this wouldn't be like an amusement park ride. This was going to be much more fun.

Whump, whump, whump.

"Hold on tight!" Lasher warned her two young riders. "If you fall, I can easily catch you in my claws. But I promise, riding in the saddle is much more comfortable."

Eli gulped. "We won't let go," he said in a shaky voice. "Will we, Grace?"

"Nope!" said Grace, happily. "Promise." She squeezed her set of reins tightly with both hands.

Before their group left for the mountain, Harvard shouted some final instructions.

"Remember, once you begin—"

"We know, Professor Harvard!" said Grace from the dragon's back. "Once we begin…"

"We must finish!" said Eli, then gave him a thumbs-up. Letting go with one hand nearly caused him to slip out of his seat, so it was a good thing they weren't very high yet.

Fireball waved too. "Have fun! And good luck finding the smigitu!" He was already selecting his letters out of the Scrabble bag. It didn't take him long to come up with his first word.

As Eli and Grace lifted higher into the air, leaving Harvard and Fireball behind to play Scrabble, they heard one last thing.

"S-I-L-V-E-R," Fireball spelled out, then placed his letters on the board. "Silver is one of the best metals to conduct electricity. It can also reflect light extremely well—just like a mirror!"

Lasher snorted. "Oh, you and that silly word game," she shouted down to her brother. "After we come back, we should all sit down and enjoy the greatest game of numbers—Yahtzee!"

Whump, whump, whump.

Lasher's wings picked up speed, and they quickly rose higher into the sky.

"This is great!" cheered Grace. "I'll bet you didn't wake up this morning and think you'd be riding a dragon for your birthday."

Eli was having fun too, even though his face looked a little green. Riding a dragon was surprisingly smooth. Sort of like riding a giant drone, except with scales, claws, and a tail that could smash huge boulders to dust.

"Woo-hoo!" cried Grace as they went higher and higher. Soon Harvard and Fireball were only tiny shapes below. Rugged mountains and golden sand dunes stretched out for miles.

"Do you see that tall mountain peak over there?" Lasher asked them, hovering in place. "The tallest one, with the shimmering entryway?"

"Yes, we see it," said Eli, feeling slightly less nauseous. "Is that where you and Fireball live?"

Lasher nodded. "That's right, Eli," she said. "Now hold old tight, okay? Here—we—go!"

Whump, whump, whump.

Lasher took off slowly, then gradually picked up speed. "I'm going slower than I normally fly," she said. "By the looks of it, Eli doesn't seem to enjoy heights very much."

Gliding through the air was fantastic! The wind whipped through their hair as they cruised over the mountaintops. The dragon was flying at over a hundred miles an hour, so the ride was over much too soon.

"Going in for a landing!" said Lasher as they quickly dropped from the sky.

Eli shut his eyes.

Below them was a large, flat area carved into the mountainside. A spot big enough for a helicopter to land—or a dragon.

THUMP.

Lasher landed on the ground much softer

when she was carrying passengers, but the ground still shook under her incredible weight.

Eli and Grace thanked her for the amazing ride, then carefully climbed down off the dragon's scaly back.

Zing!

The magical harness began to unravel so fast that it was back in the shape of a piece of string before they could ask about the return trip.

"Follow me, please!" Lasher led them on a short walk toward a tall archway that shined in the sun. A huge door made of gold, silver, and precious jewels was built right into the mountainside.

Eli whistled. "That's a fancy front door."

"Yeah, an expensive front door," said Grace. "Looks like it was made with a gazillion dollars' worth of gold and jewels." She was mostly impressed by the elaborate designs carved into the shiny metal.

Lasher used a claw to trace a secret pattern along the many lines carved into the door.

Clunk.

Something heavy moved on the inside of the mountain. It sounded like a latch being released. Then the golden door swung open.

"Welcome to my home," said Lasher, inviting them into a hollow mountain full of treasure.

11
Secret Door

When Eli and Grace stepped through the golden entrance and into the mountain, a whole new world opened up. Great tunnels were carved into the rock, with ceilings tall enough for a dragon. Gold, silver, and precious jewels were everywhere. Even the walls sparkled with diamonds.

"Wow," said Eli as they walked deeper into the mountain. Huge fireplaces carved into the walls provided plenty of light to see all the treasures. "You really live here?"

"Correct, Eli," said Lasher. "Fireball and I grew up exploring these vast halls and caves. In fact, the tunnels go so deep that even my brother and I don't know how far they go."

"Really?" Eli thought this was strange, especially since dragons live an awfully long time. "If I lived here, I would explore every little part of this place."

"Yeah, so would I," said Grace. "There's no telling what treasures are buried in here. This place is amazing!"

Lots of dragon-sized doorways opened up into the larger rooms. Most of these rooms were bigger than a school gymnasium. Each one had a large fireplace, tall paintings with gold or silver frames, and lots of antique furniture. Tables, chairs, sofas, and other fancy decorations that looked like they'd come from Uncle Larry's store.

As they kept walking, Eli and Grace also noticed a small wooden doorway up ahead. This door was just the right size for them. Instead of gold, this normal-sized door was made of thick boards. It was protected by a heavy lock, meant to guard the secrets of the mountain.

"Hey, Lasher?"

"Yes, Eli?"

"Where does that small door go?" asked Eli as they continued down the main hallway. He and his sister had to walk quickly to keep up with the speedy dragon.

Lasher stopped. "That door leads to the smaller tunnels down below the main floor," she explained, then gave a little cough. "As you can see, I'm a bit too large to fit through a door that size."

Eli grinned. "No, but we can," he said. "Grace and I can do a little *groundbreaking*." He wiggled his eyebrows. "Get it? Tunnel? Groundbreaking?"

Lasher chuckled. "Good one, Eli," she said. "But be careful with those tunnel jokes. After all, we don't want to dig ourselves too deep."

This time, Eli laughed.

Grace rolled her eyes. "Hey, at least the math dragon likes your sense of humor, Eli."

Lasher tapped a claw on her scaly chin. She seemed to be thinking very hard about something.

"I have a few things I must do at the far side of the mountain," said Lasher. "So if you two will be okay on your own for a little while, you are more than welcome to explore our home."

Eli thought that sounded like a great idea.

Grace clapped her hands. "Maybe we can find that smigitu thing that Harvard was telling us about."

Lasher laughed so deeply that it shook a handful of small diamonds off the wall.

"I think Professor Harvard may have been making up a story for our amusement," said Lasher. "I doubt very much that you will find this so-called *smigitu* anywhere in the mountain. But you are certainly welcome to try! So how about we meet back here in thirty minutes. Deal?"

"Deal," they both agreed.

Whump, whump, whump.

Lasher flapped her wings and lifted off the smooth floor. The main hallway was big enough for an airliner to land, so it was also wide enough for a dragon to fly around.

"See you in one thousand, eight hundred seconds!" said the number-loving math dragon. Then she took flight, flapping her mighty wings, and kicking up so much dust and sand that Eli and Grace had to run for cover.

Standing in front of the heavy wooden door, Eli pulled on the handle, but it wouldn't budge.

"It's locked," said Eli. "Come on, let's go explore somewhere else. There's treasure and other cool stuff to check out inside every room."

Grace rattled the keys that were still hanging around her neck. "Hold on," she said, stopping him from walking away. "Let's try one of Uncle Larry's keys and see if that works."

Click.

"Nope."

Click.

"Wrong one."

Click.

"Try again."

At some point, they'd lost count of how many keys they'd tried. Until by chance…

Clunk.

Grace found the right key. The heavy latch released, and the door swung open all on its own.

Creeeeeeeak.

Behind the door was a staircase carved right into the mountain, spiraling down, down, down.

12
In Too Deep

"Nice job, Grace!" Eli slapped his sister a hi-five. "I would have given up a long time ago."

Grace shrugged it off. "Thanks. I guess little sisters have more patience than big brothers."

Together, they headed down the stone steps, slow and steady, so neither of them tripped. They looped around, and around, and around.

"HEY!" shouted Grace, enjoying the sound of her voice as it bounced off the walls.

*Hey…hey…hey…*went the echo.

Eli jumped from the sudden loud noise. "Don't do that!" he said, grabbing his chest. "Or at least warn me first."

Grace giggled. "Sorry. I just wanted to hear the echo."

After what felt like walking down a thousand steps, they finally reached the end. At the bottom of the spiral staircase was a wide open room. The walls were carved from solid rock, but it looked like somebody's work room. There was a table, a chair, and some measuring equipment. There were several types of magnifying glasses, a microscope, and an antique set of scales with an orange price tag that read: **$29 (OBO)**.

Eli shrugged. "Must be somebody's office," he said. "I'll bet whoever works down here uses this stuff to test out all those colorful gems and diamonds we saw earlier."

Torches hung on the walls, so there was plenty of light. But Grace had a sneaky feeling there was something a bit odd about them.

Tap, tap, tap.

"Yep, they're plastic," said Grace. "Professor Harvard must have fixed this place up."

"I'll bet there's electricity running through

this whole mountain," said Eli. "A state-of-the-art mountain house."

Sand crunched under their feet as they ventured farther into the room. Hardly a few steps away from the staircase—

Slam!

A stone door slid shut behind them.

"Hey, wait!" Eli rushed back and pounded on the door, but it was too late.

They were trapped.

"Lasher! We're down here!" cried Eli. "Get us out of here!" He was so busy yelling for help that he didn't hear the strange noise coming from the other side of the room.

Grace tapped her brother's shoulder. "Um, Eli? I think we have a bigger problem."

The room was filling up with gemstones. Dark green emeralds, bright red rubies, and sapphires of purple, blue, and even pink and orange.

Plink-plink-plink-plink-plink.

In less than a minute, they were buried up to their ankles in precious gems. The stones poured into the room from an opening in the wall. A chute as big as a playground slide kept dumping the jewels like an avalanche. And it didn't sound like it was going to stop anytime soon.

Eli and Grace quickly realized they were in serious trouble. This was no ordinary room for checking the carat, clarity, color, and cut of precious gems.

They were trapped inside a vault.

13
Balancing Act

The room was going to fill up long before they figured out a plan. Gemstones came pouring down the chute so fast that soon the entire floor was covered in colorful stones, big and small.

"Quick!" shouted Eli. "Check the walls! Look everywhere!" His head darted left and right, searching all around. "There must be some kind of button or secret lever."

"Okay, I'll check this side," Grace shouted over the noise. "You check over there."

As fast as they could, they patted their hands along the rough wall, searching for a way out. A button, switch, or any kind of clue about how to escape.

"Anything?" asked Eli. "A secret lever?"

"Nothing," said Grace, sounding worried. "We're running out of time, Eli. Maybe there is no secret button. It could be something else we haven't thought of yet."

"Like what?" said Eli, trying to keep the panic out of his voice. That was difficult to do when trapped inside a room that was filling with precious stones.

Grace threw her hands in the air. "I don't know!" she said. "But we better figure it out fast."

Clink-clink-clink-clink-clink-clink-clink.

Eli scanned the room, looking for any kind of hint. Besides the chute that kept dumping all the gems into the room, the only other thing in sight was the work table with all the measuring equipment.

"Wait a second—" Eli kept staring at all the gemology tools. "Grace, hold on. That scale must be here for a reason. Maybe we have to figure out the right measurement to stop the room from filling up."

Plink-plink-plink-plink-plink-plink-plink.

"Quick!" shouted Eli. "Up on the table!"

"What?" Grace shook her head. "That's not going to do any good. We can't just sit in one spot while this room fills up."

"I have an idea!" shouted Eli.

Crunch, crunch, crunch.

Working together, the two of them made it over to the table. But with all the measuring equipment, there was only enough room for one person.

Grace sat crisscross on the table, while gems continued to pile up all around them.

"I knew it!" Eli showed his sister the clue. Etched into one side of the scale was the letter E, for Eli. The other side was etched with a capital G, for Grace.

"Okay, great," said Grace. "Now what?"

Eli searched the table, but there was nothing but the gemology tools: microscope, magnifying glass, tweezers, calipers, color charts, and a bunch of supplies for cleaning and polishing.

"Check the drawer," suggested Grace, pointing to the small handle that was nearly buried.

"Got it!" Eli ripped open the drawer and found a lined index card with words printed on it.

"There's a note," he said. "It looks like some kind of math problem."

When a young boy turned four years old, his sister was half his age. Now that the older brother has just turned ten... How old is the younger sister?

Each of them were quiet while they studied the riddle for a moment. Both of them knew that math puzzles sometimes had the answer hidden inside the question.

"That's easy!" said Eli. "Half of ten is five." He quickly scooped up a handful of gems. He didn't have to reach very far because he was already buried up to his waist. He placed ten gems on his side of the scale, and five on Grace's side.

They waited, but nothing happened.

"That can't be right," said Grace. "If the boy is four years old, and the girl is half his age…she'd be two years old, right?"

"Yeah," agreed Eli. "Half of four is two."

"But when you get older," Grace went on, "that doesn't change. You're two years older than me, and you always will be."

"Okay, so…" Eli had to trick his brain into not making the math equation seem more difficult. But it was hard to concentrate with the noise of the gemstones pouring into the room. "That would make the girl eight years old."

Grace changed the number of gems on her side of the scale to eight.

Clink…clink…clink.

The gems were slowing down! It took a moment for them to stop completely, but soon the chute stopped sending millions of precious stones into the room.

Shoop!

A secret door just big enough for them to squeeze through suddenly opened up in the wall. They'd worked together and discovered the way out.

"You did it!" cheered Eli.

"You mean *we* did it," said Grace. "You figured out the part about using the scale. All I did was figure out a silly math riddle."

Eli laughed. "Yeah, I guess I was overthinking that one a little bit." He could relax now that they were out of danger. "Come on, let's go see where the secret door leads to."

14
Silver Lining

Eli and Grace had to crawl, creep, and drag each other across the room full of gems once more to get to the open doorway. It was much easier when they weren't under so much pressure, and their hearts weren't racing so fast.

Eli made it across first. "Let's get back upstairs and find out where—" He stopped. "Wait a second. This doesn't look like the way out."

Grace stood up and joined him, brushing precious gems off her clothes. She didn't like what she saw either.

"You're right," she said. "This looks more like a spooky tunnel to nowhere."

A long, narrow hallway was carved into the mountain. It reached high above their heads. So much light was shining down that it was too bright to tell where it came from. The sun? Solar panels? A million flashlights?

Behind them was nothing but solid rock. Ahead of them was a V-shaped pathway that twisted and turned so much that it was impossible to see what lay ahead.

"Should we check it out?" asked Eli.

Grace wasn't sure it was a good idea. She also didn't see any other option. "I guess we have to see where it goes," she said. "It's our only choice." She gave her brother a little push and told him to go first.

Eli smiled weakly. "Gee, thanks."

Taking slow, careful steps, they made their way along the rocky path. Some parts were narrower than others, so they had to place their hands on the jagged wall to keep their balance.

"You okay back there?" asked Eli, then nearly tripped over his own feet.

"Yes, I'm okay," said Grace. "I just wish this path was a little wider. It's almost too small for me!"

Rounding corner after corner, turn after turn, it felt like they'd been walking for miles.

"Hey, I see something!" Eli hurried toward the shiny object. "Check this out! I think we just found our next clue."

A silver plate was leaning up against the wall, as if waiting to be discovered. Etched into the metal was their second math problem.

$$8 + 6 = 2$$
How is this possible?

Eli turned to his sister. "Do you get it?"

Grace shook her head. "No, but I think we need to figure it out—*fast*." She pointed to the wall, where a series of holes were opening up.

Shoop! Shoop! Shoop!

None of the holes were wide enough to escape through. Just big enough for more treasure to come piling into the narrow corridor.

Clang.

Silver plates, silver cups, silver bowls, and a million other silver treasures came pouring down. Judging by how fast they were piling up, clanging and banging down on top of each other, it wouldn't take long to fill the whole place up to the top—with them at the bottom.

"Not good," said Grace, nervously.

"Definitely not good," said Eli, backing up. With his eyes wide with fear, he grabbed his sister's hand, then shouted one word: "RUN!"

15

Time to Reflect

When they were finally able to put some distance between them and the falling treasures, Eli and Grace slowed to a walk. The noise of the silver storm was growing fainter with each step.

The corridor twisted, turned, and changed directions so many times that it was impossible to tell what was around the next corner.

Eli led the way, staying focused on the pathway in front of him. What popped up next caused him to stop so suddenly that his sister crashed into him.

"Oh, great," complained Eli. "A dead end."

Instead of solid rock, there was a tall clock built right into the wall. It looked similar to a grandfather clock, but without a glass front to show off the *pendulum*, the part that counted off the seconds and minutes. The clock was painted dark green, though the colors had faded over time.

Eli stood on his tiptoes to read the orange price tag sticker that was at the top.

Swedish Mora Clock
$12,999.00 (1850s)

The clock had regular numbers instead of roman numerals, so it was easy to read. The hands were stuck at exactly 12 o'clock.

Clang.

Grace jumped. "What was that?"

Eli wiped his sweaty forehead. "That's the sound of a million silver plates, bowls, and teapots coming this way."

After searching everywhere for a secret lever

and finding nothing, they tried yelling for help. But there was no way Lasher could hear them way down here.

The noises were getting much closer.

"Check the clue again," suggested Grace. "There has to be a way out of here."

Eli held up the silver plate with the math problem engraved in the center.

$$8 + 6 = 2$$

How is this possible?

Eli shook his head. "It's *not* possible," he said. "Last time I checked, eight plus six equals fourteen. Not two."

More and more silver antiques kept piling up behind them. The holes where the treasures were pouring out of were getting closer too.

"Oh no," groaned Eli. "Look!"

When the silver storm finally caught up to them, they had to tilt their heads back.

A mountain of silver rose up and out of sight. With the bright light shining down, the glare made it hard to see how high it reached. And it was getting closer with each passing second.

Clink-clink-clink-clink-clink.

What little bit of time they had to solve the math puzzle was almost up. It would take Lasher forever to dig them out. And that's if she even knew where to look.

"Okay, think…" Grace tried to calculate the math equation forward, backward, and every other way she could dream up. But it just didn't make sense.

"Eight plus six equals two…*somehow*," said Grace, trying to ignore the noise and clatter all around them. "We just need to think about it a different way. Any ideas?"

"NO! I'm all out of ideas!" Eli spun around in circles, getting more and more frustrated. "What are we going to do?" He kept throwing his arms in the air and waving the silver plate around, as if he could fly them out of this mess.

"Eli, wait!" Grace pointed to the clock. "You just moved the clock—somehow."

The minute hand of the antique clock was no longer stuck at twelve o'clock.

12: 05

"Do that again," said Grace.

"Do what? You mean do this?" Eli flapped his arms like he'd done before. He felt foolish, but it caused the hands on the clock to move again.

Tick-tick-tick-tick-tick.

12: 10

"We did it!" Grace jumped up and down. "That has to be the answer!"

Eli gave an exasperated sigh. "What's it?" he said. "What are you talking about?"

Grace pointed to the clue written on the silver plate. "Time!" she said. "That's the answer to the equation. Eight plus six equals two! Get it?"

Eli stopped to think about it. He had to count on his fingers to make sure. "Nine, ten, eleven, twelve o'clock…" His eyes lit up.

"One o'clock, two o'clock," finished Grace. "See? It's a math riddle about time."

Both of them were happy to have figured out the answer, but there was no time to celebrate. Mounds of silver had already piled up behind them. The mountain of treasure was growing higher and higher with every wasted second.

"Eli, hurry!" said Grace.

Eli tried to force the hands of the clock around so they would land on two o'clock, but they wouldn't budge.

"I can't move them," said Eli. "They're stuck."

Clang. Clang. Clang.

Silver antiques kept crashing down all around them. Every time they tossed one out of the way, three more would quickly take its place.

"Hey, wait a minute—" Grace wiggled her lips back and forth, thinking really hard. "Didn't Fireball say something about silver?"

Eli was busy tossing antique silver plates like frisbees, trying to give them more room. "Yeah, something about how silver is really good at reflecting light…"

Instantly, their eyes lit up when they recalled what Fireball had mentioned earlier.

"Silver is one of the best metals to conduct electricity. It can also reflect light extremely well."

"It's working!" Grace used the light from above to shine a beam of reflected light directly at the face of the clock. Slowly, the hands on the clock spun around toward the right answer—2 o'clock.

"Yeah, it's working," said Eli. "But not fast enough." He kept shoving treasures out of the way, but it didn't help. "Keep going, Grace. I'll try to keep this mountain of silver out of the way."

DING!

DING!

A loud chime rang out when the clock hands finally settled on two o'clock.

"Done!" said Grace. "Now what?" She was worried they'd come up with the wrong answer.

At the last moment, right before they were buried with forks, spoons, and butter knives made of sterling silver, the clock opened up to reveal a secret door.

Grace jumped through. "Eli, come on!" Her mouth fell open when she saw the pile of silver antiques that had to be at least fifty feet high. It looked ready to collapse.

"Grace, help me!" said Eli. "I can't move! My foot is stuck!" He reached out his hand, weaving his arm through the tiny gaps in the mountain of treasure that had him buried up to his chin.

Grace pulled as hard as she could. "Eli!"

CRASH!

Falling backward, they landed in a pile on the stone floor. The secret door squeaked shut behind them, cutting off the sound of a silver avalanche.

16
Spinning Gold

After picking themselves up off the floor, Eli and Grace got their first look around. Sunlight was shining down from above, providing more than enough light to see they were inside another room.

A thick stone wall surrounded them on all sides, forming a large circle. Carved into the stone wall were ten archways, each one leading to another smaller room—or possibly a way out.

"See anything over there?" asked Eli, peeking into another room. He hadn't seen a doorway, a ladder they could use to climb out, or any sign of an exit.

"Nope," said Grace, still checking the rooms on the other side. "These are empty too. Except for all the gold."

Ten large rooms, each one filled to the tipping point with piles of treasure. Gold bars, gold coins, gold jewelry, and statues made of pure gold.

"I wonder what one of these gold coins is worth," said Eli, searching his last room.

"Or a gazillion of them," joked Grace, stepping over a pile of gold coins to check her last room.

When they'd finished looking for a way out, they met back in the center of the main room.

"What do we do now?" Grace asked her brother. "All these rooms are blocked."

Eli scanned the area again. "I guess the only thing we can do is search for another clue," he said. "There has to be something we missed."

Each of them got busy searching every inch of the main room. No gold was pouring into the room, so they could relax for a moment.

"Hey, that was good thinking back there," said Eli as he ran his hand along the wall, checking for anything out of the ordinary. "When Mount Silver was about to topple over, I started to panic a little bit."

"Ha!" Grace glanced over her shoulder at her brother. "A little?"

Eli grinned. "Okay, a lot." He picked up one of the gold coins at his feet. There were no words or engravings. Just a picture of a dragon.

"Hey, this one looks like Lasher," said Eli, showing off the coin in his hand.

Grace picked one up too. "Yeah, and this one kind of looks like—" She stared in disbelief, then tossed the coin to her brother.

Eli recognized who it was immediately. "An Uncle Larry coin!" he said with a laugh. "It looks just like him."

Grace's smile disappeared. "I hope he's okay," she said. "Wherever he is…"

"I'm sure he's fine," Eli reassured her. "You heard what Professor Harvard said. He told us that Uncle Larry was taking some time off."

After searching the walls for some kind of

hint, Eli accidentally came across exactly what they were looking for. When his shoe caught on something, he used his foot to sweep away the rocks and sand to reveal some hidden numbers on the floor.

"Um, Grace?"

Grace turned to see her brother staring at the ground. He was waving at her to come over. "Did you find something?" she asked, then hurried over to join him.

Eli pointed at the floor. "I think I found our clue. Any idea how to solve it?"

Grace kneeled down and traced her fingers along the grooves carved into the stone. She swept away the remaining mess to reveal the rest of the puzzle.

$$6 + 4 = 4$$

Make this statement true.

(Use one move only)

The room was eerily quiet. No sea of gems came pouring into the room, and no pile of silver threatening to bury them.

Clink.

They both froze when they heard the familiar sound of growing wealth.

First it was just a few gold coins shifting around. Then a few more, and a few more, until the sound was coming from every room.

Plink-plink-plink-plink-plink.

"Here we go again," said Eli. "Whoa!" He nearly lost his balance when something else happened that he didn't expect.

The room was spinning! Slowly at first, then gradually picking up more speed.

"Oh, great," said Grace. "This time we have to solve the math puzzle while moving."

Eli knelt next to his sister. He was the first to realize what was happening.

"Not just moving," he said. "We're sinking. Look! The archways are getting taller."

What they'd been staring at was only the tops of the archways. As the room spun around, the archways grew taller as they continued to drop. The deeper they sank into the heart of the mountain, the more the huge piles of gold came sliding into the room.

With *them* at the center.

17
Grindstone

The piles of gold continued to spill across the floor, closing in all around them. Gold coins formed a circle around Eli and Grace as they tried to solve the math riddle.

"These math puzzles are hard enough," said Eli. "Now we have to solve this one while going around in circles!"

The entire room continued to spin in a counterclockwise direction, taking them deeper into the mountain.

"AHH!" Grace jumped when it felt like something jumped into her pocket. Her magic junk—the tiny screwdriver bit—had changed into something much larger.

An engraver.

"It doesn't work," said Grace, flicking the button on and off. "Maybe it needs to be charged. Or else it needs—"

"Batteries!" Eli's magic junk didn't need to change into something else to become useful. Two triple-A batteries were exactly what they needed.

"Hurry, put them in." Grace pried open the slot where the batteries went. "No, the other way."

"Sorry." Eli flipped the batteries around.

Bzzzzzzzzt.

The engraver came to life!

"Okay, it works," said Eli. "Now what?" They were still spinning around and around while the pile of gold grew bigger and bigger. If they didn't solve it soon, the equation itself would be buried underneath all the gold.

$$6 + 4 = 4$$

"This one isn't like the last math puzzle," said Grace, reading the equation several times. "I think we literally have to move the numbers."

"Yeah, but which number?" said Eli. "We only have one move. One chance to get it right."

Grace studied the numbers. "What if we cross out the last four and make it ten," she suggested. "That would make the equation true, right? Six plus four equals ten."

Eli shook his head. "I don't think we're allowed to cross out a number," he said. "See how each number is made of individual lines? I think we can only change one part of a number, not the whole thing."

Grace's shoulders slumped. "Oh. Right."

Gold pieces continued to pile up all around them. They had to fight off the growing treasure, shoveling it away so the gold wouldn't completely bury the math riddle they were trying to solve.

Eli shifted his foot to move closer. "What about…" He reached out a hand, then stopped. "No, that won't work. What if we try…"

"ELI!" shouted Grace, making him jump.

"What's wrong?" Eli thought a mountain of gold coins was about to come crashing down.

"Your shoe!" cheered Grace. "Your foot just figured out the answer!"

Eli dropped his gaze to where she was pointing. His left shoe had blocked out one small piece of the first number in the equation, so now it looked more like a 5 instead of a 6.

Grace used the engraver to smooth over one section of the first number. But now they had to add a line to the last number.

"Are there any more pieces?" asked Eli. "Maybe it's like Dad's screwdriver at home, the one with all the extra stuff inside."

"Good idea." Grace unscrewed the cap off the engraver. Several more bits fell out. They had to dig through the pile of gold coins to find them.

"Try that one," suggested Eli. "The pointy one."

Grace fumbled a few times because she was so nervous, but finally locked in the sharp bit that would hopefully carve into solid stone.

Plink-plink-plink-plink-plink.

Eli used his hands and feet to brush the treasures out of the way, so his sister could keep working. Gold rings, gold medallions, and gold nuggets threatened to stop them from getting the right answer engraved into the stone in time.

"You're doing great!" cheered Eli. "Don't stop, keep going!"

Grace's hands were shaking. She was breathing heavily, worried it wasn't going to work. But she finally managed to get one line carved into the stone. With one move, just like the riddle said, they had managed to make the equation true.

Now the numbers read:

$$5 + 4 = 9$$

When the correct number was engraved in the stone, the entire floor stopped spinning.

But the ride wasn't over. The larger part of the room stopped rotating, allowing the middle part to break away.

"Hold on!" said Eli. "We're not done yet."

Now they were going up. Way, *way* up.

Now only the middle section was moving, with them hunched down right in the center.

"Eli?" said Grace, nervously. She gripped her brother so tight that he winced in pain.

"I've gotcha," said Eli, trying to sound brave even though he was scared too. "I think we're going back up to the top. Just hold on, okay? It'll be over in a minute—I hope."

A ten-foot stone circle was rising up from the middle of the huge gold *depository*, a giant room used to store an incredible amount of gold—a dragon's treasure.

Eli imagined it was just like being inside one of Uncle Larry's cheap pens that he always gave to customers. As if they were sitting on top of a giant plastic ink chamber, while rising through the barrel of the world's biggest ballpoint pen.

Grace squeezed her eyes shut.

Eli held his sister tight and stayed right in the center, not daring to move, or else risk falling off the edge.

18
A Friendly Face

When the ride was over, it took a moment for Eli and Grace to realize they were back inside the main entrance. The pillar of stone they were riding had slid into place on the top floor, not far from where they'd started.

Eli tapped his sister on the shoulder. "You can open your eyes now," he told her. "We're back in the main hallway, where Lasher dropped us off."

Just a short walk down the enormous hall was the door they'd first gone through when Lasher flew off to do some errands on the other side of the mountain.

"Do you hear that?" Eli looked up and down the hallway, but saw no one else around.

Grace heard it too.

Voices.

"Come on," said Grace. "I think it's coming from in there." She was already walking toward the room on the far side of the hallway, with the door wide open.

It was hard to believe they were still inside a mountain. The room itself looked like a normal office. An antique table took up most of the room, surrounded by a bunch of slightly used office chairs. In the middle of the table, facing the opposite direction, was a laptop.

As soon as they gazed out the windows…

"Wow," said Eli, breathlessly.

"Yeah, no kidding," said Grace, equally impressed. "Actually, I don't think *wow* is a big enough word to describe this."

The view was amazing!

Eli and Grace stumbled toward the window with their mouths hanging open. Eyes wide, they stared through the thick glass, taking in the incredible view of the hollow mountain.

"Look at all that gold!" said Eli, sticking his nose right up to the glass.

"And silver," said Grace. "And gems. And look at that huge pile of diamonds over there!"

Stretching out across the length of several soccer fields were riches beyond belief. More precious stones, more silver, and more gold than they ever thought possible.

A voice whispered, "*Pssssssst*! Over here!"

The view from the mountain office was truly magnificent. Eli and Grace had never seen anything like it. But they were even more thrilled to see the smiling face staring back at them from the screen of the laptop sitting on the table.

It was Uncle Larry.

19
Teacher's Aide

Grace rushed over to the table, pulling the laptop closer so they could both see him better. "Uncle Larry! Is that really you?"

Eli waved to the tiny image of Uncle Larry, who was smiling back at them from inside a tiny square on the screen.

"Hi, Uncle Larry!" Eli felt a huge smile spread across his face. "It's great to see you! How are you?"

Grace crinkled her nose. "And *where* are you? Are you having some kind of business meeting?"

Each box on the screen was filled with the

faces of all their teachers from their past junkyard adventures. They were all chatting away, but their voices were on mute. And most of them were in a different place.

The art monster was in his studio.

The alien of astronomy was in his spaceship, joining the meeting from outer space.

The mummy of medicine was in his office, leaning back in his chair with his bandaged feet up on the desk.

The giant of geography was at a park somewhere, with tall mountains in the distance.

The gargoyle of geometry was inside his castle, talking to another teacher while Mo and Lem circled around him, causing mischief.

The weather witch was at home, streaming from her living room.

The mermaid of music and the sea serpent of science were both there too, attending the online meeting from the Underwater Academy.

"My very first meeting!" said Uncle Larry proudly. "I'm going to be a teacher's aide!"

Eli and Grace congratulated him on his new job, but also realized what this meant. That Uncle Larry wasn't going to be running the store any longer.

"What about the adventures?" asked Grace.

"Yeah, we can't go on junkyard adventures without you," said Eli, just as concerned as his sister. "Who's going to run the antique store?"

The room went quiet for a moment.

On the screen, Uncle Larry raised both index fingers and pointed directly at them.

"You are, of course!" said Uncle Larry. "You two have been on enough junkyard adventures to know how it works. Now you can help all those other kids get set up, show them where to go, and hand out all the magic junk they'll need."

"Or join them?" asked Grace, sounding hopeful.

"Yes, even better!" said Uncle Larry. "And besides, you don't need me around all the time. You'll have Professor Harvard there to help if you ever run into trouble."

Eli wondered about something else. "But how is that going to work, Uncle Larry? You can't just give us your store. Can you?"

Uncle Larry wiggled his bushy eyebrows. "You bet I can!" he said with a grin. "All the necessary paperwork has been filed. Just have your dad read it over, then sign on the dotted line." He gave them a thumbs-up. "And you already have the keys!"

Eli and Grace sat there in shock. They were still trying to wrap their heads around what Uncle Larry was telling them. That the Antique Shop & Junkyard was changing owners.

The store now belonged to *them*.

"Well, it was great to see you both," said Uncle Larry. "But I need to get back to my meeting. I just wanted to say a quick hello, then show you the way out." He pointed off to the left side, but that was the entrance they'd just walked through. Then he pointed the other way. "Sorry, I meant the *other* left."

A regular door was at the far end of the room, with four rectangular panels cut out, and a simple brass door knob.

Uncle Larry asked, "Do you see it?"

"Yeah, we see it," said Eli.

"Is that the way back?" asked Grace.

Uncle Larry nodded. "That door will take you back to the store," he explained. "To your brand-new, *er*—I mean, *used* antique store. But before you go, the other teachers and I would like you to do one more thing..."

Eli and Grace listened carefully as Uncle Larry explained the plan that he, Professor Harvard, and all the other teachers came up with to get the word dragon and the math dragon to stop fighting all the time.

"It might not stop them from arguing completely," said Uncle Larry, "but that amazing old antique might provide a good enough distraction. Everyone agrees that it's time for those two dragons to quit their foolish bickering, get back to work, and start taking kids on junkyard adventures once again. You'll find it over there behind you. I put it in one of those cupboard thingys over there—uh, somewhere."

Much too soon, their visit was over.

"Bye, Uncle Larry!" said Eli.

"Have fun at your new job!" said Grace.

Uncle Larry gave one final wave, smiling hugely, revealing that familiar sparkle behind his greenish-yellow eyes. He fumbled a bit with the keyboard, then the laptop screen went blank.

It took them a while to find it, since Uncle Larry forgot where he'd put it. But they finally found the special item in one of the drawers underneath the gold-trimmed countertops.

The astrolabe.

Before Eli and Grace could come up with any kind of plan, a huge shadow spread across the room.

A deep voice said, "There you are."

Eli and Grace turned around to see a large, scaly head peeking in the doorway.

Lasher was back.

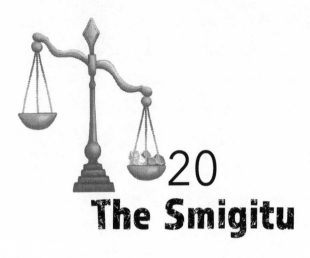

20
The Smigitu

The math dragon's green eyes were already focused on the astrolabe. Lasher was extremely curious about the object that Eli was holding.

"Here you go, Lasher," said Eli, then offered the astrolabe to his new dragon friend. "It's a gift from me and my sister. We thought you and Fireball could figure it out together."

"It's the smigitu!" cheered Grace.

Lasher leaned in close to see it better. Eli and Grace could feel the dragon's hot breath as she studied the curious object that was inscribed with letters, numbers, and all sorts of strange markings.

"Today is your birthday, Eli," said Lasher. "And you are offering *me* this valuable gift?"

Eli acted like it was no big deal. "The astro—" He stopped when his sister nudged him. "I mean, the smigitu can do all sorts of amazing stuff. You can use it to figure out the time of day, when the sun will set, or when the moon will rise."

"And navigate the seas!" said Grace.

"And measure the height of a mountain."

"And study the stars at night."

Lasher made a noise in her throat. "The stars?" Her eyes grew wide as she carefully used her sharp claws to grab the astrolabe—the *smigitu*—from Eli's outstretched hand.

They tried not to laugh at the way the math dragon stared at the small object, completely mesmerized, as if the astrolabe truly was the single most incredible gizmo in the universe.

"Thank you," said Lasher. "My brother and I may not agree on everything, since he loves words so much and I have a passion for numbers and math. But ever since we were young, we would spend days...months...even years gazing up at the stars. Which, as you know, truly have no equivalent."

Eli and Grace agreed that words are great, and so are numbers. But the secrets of the universe were so vast, so amazing, so limitless, that nobody could deny that.

"Eli? Grace? Where are you?"

Everyone was surprised when a familiar voice echoed down into the meeting room.

"Uh-oh," said Grace. "It's Dad."

Their dad was calling to them from behind the door that Uncle Larry told them to use to get back to the store.

Lasher was disappointed they couldn't stay to work on some more math puzzles. "I suppose it's time for you two to head back," the dragon said. "After all, you have a birthday party to get ready for." She winked one purple eye.

Eli and Grace were both sad to leave, but even the best adventures had to end at some point.

"Bye, Lasher!" said Grace, waving over her

shoulder. "It was nice to meet you!"

"See ya, Lasher!" said Eli. "I hope you and Fireball have fun with the smigitu!"

Lasher the math dragon thanked them for the gift, and told them how she couldn't wait to show the smigitu to her brother, so they could start to figure out everything it could do.

Thump, thump, thump, thump, thump.

Together, Eli and Grace hurried up the staircase, smiling about their adventure, but also excited to get back to the store. But when they reached the top of the long staircase, the exit was blocked.

21
A New Adventure

"Dad! We're in here!" Eli pounded his fists on the solid wood barrier. They were stuck behind what appeared to be an antique bookshelf. Tiny slivers of light peeked through the gaps and cracks, so at least they could see inside the store. They just couldn't get there.

"Hold on," said Dad, somewhere on the other side. "I have to move this—"

Creeeeeeak.

"—old bookshelf out—"

Squeeeeak.

"—of the way."

It sounded like their dad was really struggling to move the heavy bookshelf. With all his effort, pushing and pulling, lifting and shoving, the bulky bookshelf had hardly moved an inch.

From the other side, their dad shouted, "Let me catch my breath…then I'll…try again."

Eli felt all over the place to figure out why the door was stuck. "Oh," he said, feeling a bit silly. "No wonder why we're stuck. There's a lock right here."

Grace jiggled the lanyard still hanging around her neck. "I have just the thing for that," she said. "Somewhere in this mess of keys."

With only a tiny bit of light peeking through the holes in the bookshelf, they both tried to figure out which key to use. There were at least a hundred different keys to choose from.

"That one?"

"No."

"What about that one?"

"No."

"It's got to be this one," said Grace, then jammed a rusty old skeleton key into the lock.

Click.

Light from the store poured into the dim stairwell. Eli and Grace both leapt out and wrapped their arms around their dad, squeezing him so tight that he nearly dropped the official documents he was holding.

Now that Eli and Grace were safe, there was something important they needed to talk about.

"Eli? Grace?" Dad had a stern look on his face. Not mad, just concerned. "Did you two have something to do with this?"

Dad held up the stack or papers.

"I found these documents on the front counter when I was ready to check out," explained Dad. "This is a transfer of ownership. A quitclaim deed, basically. A sole proprietorship with our names written on it."

Eli and Grace weren't old enough to know exactly what their dad was talking about, but it sounded like Uncle Larry wasn't joking.

The antique store really had changed owners.

All the necessary papers and documents were signed, initialed, and made perfectly legal.

A shadow appeared behind them.

First it was dog-shaped, then human.

Harvard was back!

"I'm afraid it's all true," said Harvard, coming swiftly around the corner. "The store now belongs to your family."

"How did you—?" Their dad only caught a glimpse of Harvard changing shape. Just enough to confuse him so that he could hardly speak.

Harvard pretended not to understand what all the fuss was about. "Yes, Ben?"

"But—? You were just—?" mumbled their dad, unsure of what he'd just witnessed. All he could do was shake his head, thinking he must have imagined seeing a dog change into a human.

Those types of things did *not* happen.

Not unless magic was *real*, of course.

"This way, family!" said Harvard. "Let's get all your party supplies packed up, shall we?"

Everyone grabbed a bag to carry, then Harvard walked them out to the car. Except for the cake, their dad had found everything they needed on their party supply list. Even a small hand pump, so he could blow up all those balloons without getting a headache.

With everything loaded up, Eli and Grace climbed into the back seat. They got buckled while Professor Harvard spoke privately to their dad. Through the window, they could only make out bits and pieces of the conversation.

"Don't worry, Ben…"

"…can't run a store…"

"…with my help…"

"But—? But—?"

"…Eli and Grace too…"

A moment later, Dad climbed into the driver's seat and started the engine. He took a moment to collect his thoughts, then said, "Ready, troops?"

"Ready," they both said.

Eli howled, "Let's party!"

Grace hollered, "Woo-hoo!"

Driving down Broadway Street on a busy Saturday morning, feeling good about their latest junkyard adventure, Eli and Grace spoke in hushed voices in the back seat. They couldn't help but laugh to themselves about their good fortune.

"What are you two giggling about back there?" asked Dad as he made a right turn. They pulled into the parking lot of the cake shop, which would be their last stop before heading home.

"Oh, nothing," said Eli.

"Just talking," said Grace.

Dad parked the car and shut off the engine. "Let me guess…" He turned around to face them. "All your laughing and whispering doesn't have anything to do with the fact that we now own an antique store, does it?"

Eli and Grace tried their best to look innocent, but it was too hard to hide their excitement.

Their dad let out a big sigh. But even he couldn't hide the smile on his face.

"We'll talk about it tomorrow," said Dad. "Right now, we have a party to get ready for. Let's grab the birthday cake, then we'll head home to blow up some balloons." He hopped out of the car and waited for them to join him on the sidewalk.

In the backseat, Eli wiggled his eyebrows at his sister, who was grinning back at him. They were both thinking the same thing. From here on out, they didn't need an excuse to go to Uncle Larry's store—to *their* store. And they didn't need to ask…*Can we go too?*

Junkyard Adventures belonged to them now. And they could go whenever, wherever, and with whoever they wanted. Friends from school, friends from clubs, and new friends from the neighborhood…who were all invited to the party.

Thank you for reading Book 10 of the **Junkyard Adventures** series. I hope you enjoyed visiting Uncle Larry's Antique Shop & Junkyard.

If you have time to leave a review, I would appreciate it! If you want to go on more adventures with Eli and Grace, please check out the other JYA books.

Follow the Author

Sign up for my newsletter to receive all the latest books and news at:

www.TevinHansen.com

Dear Eli and Grace,

Thank you so much for helping my brother and I settle our long-lasting argument about numbers and words. We have finally agreed they are both equally important.

I heard from Professor Harvard that our dear Uncle Larry has taken up a teacher's aide position at the Underwater Academy.

And I also understand that the store now belongs to your family. That is excellent news! I'm sure you will have many more adventures during the weeks, months, and years to come. Congratulations!

Uncle Larry's keys will unlock all the secret doors — including the ones inside the mountain.

Dragons do not have much use for treasure. We are having too much fun with our new gift!

My brother and I wish to thank you very much for the astrolabe. It truly is the single most incredible gizmo in the universe. Although, now that we have been using the astrolabe to learn more about the universe, we've been having a rather heated argument about which is better...the sun or the moon.

I hope to see you again soon!

Your friend,
Lasher.

PS — There are many adventures out there, so be careful, work together, and learn as much as you can. And don't forget that once you begin...
You must finish.

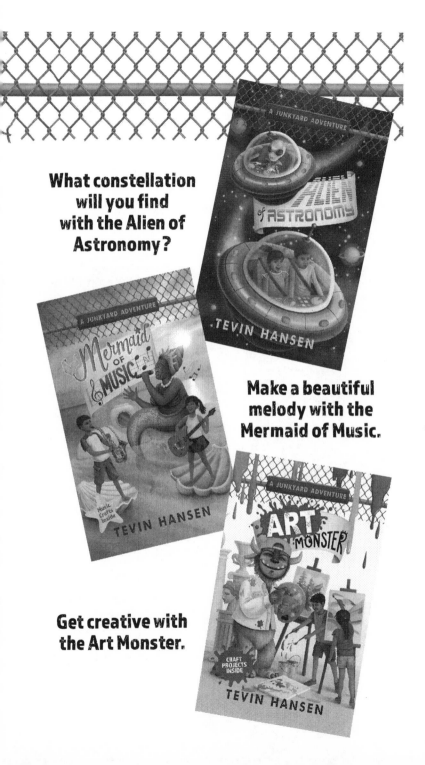

63904221R00079